# Pearlie
## and the
## Lost Handbag

**WENDY HARMER**

Illustrated by Mike Zarb

RANDOM HOUSE AUSTRALIA

For Josephine and Rosalind

Random House Australia Pty Ltd
Level 3, 100 Pacific Highway, North Sydney NSW 2060
http://www.randomhouse.com.au
Sydney   New York   Toronto
London   Auckland   Johannesburg
First published by Random House Australia 2005

National Library of Australia
Cataloguing-in-Publication Entry

Harmer, Wendy.
Pearlie and the lost handbag.
For lower primary school aged children.
ISBN 978 1 74166 102 6.
ISBN 1 74166 102 1.
1. Fairies – Juvenile fiction. I. Zarb, Michael.
II. Title.
A823.3

Designed and typeset by Jobi Murphy
Printed and bound by Everbest Printing Co. Ltd, China

It was a warm, sunny Tuesday afternoon in Jubilee Park. The small children had gone home to have a sleep and the big people had gone back to work after eating their lunch under the shady trees.

Pearlie the park fairy loved
this time of day when it was
peaceful. She flew around
with the sun sparkling on her
wings making sure that
everything was tidy and in
its place, just right!

Pearlie was on her way back
to her shell on the old stone
fountain to have some
afternoon tea when she noticed
a sign stuck to a lamppost.

And this is what
the sign said:

Lost handbag

Red leather with
white spots

Last seen near
the pond

Reward

Ring Mrs Brown
0044 0044

'Buds and blossoms,' said Pearlie, 'I know that spotty handbag. It belongs to that kind old lady who comes to feed the ducks every day. It won't be long before the gates are closed for the night. I'd better look for this lost handbag right now.' And she whizzed off as fast as she could go.

Well, Pearlie searched high and low. She started looking near the pond. She looked up in branches and down under rocks, behind bushes and in front of the rubbish bins, all around the roundabout and back and forth across the playground. But she didn't see a spotty red bag anywhere at all.

Pearlie decided to call together all the creatures who lived in Jubilee Park to ask whether any of them had found the handbag. She tinkled the pearls on her magic wand, and one by one they arrived at the bottom of the fountain.

'Excuse me, everyone,' said Pearlie, 'I need your help. Kind Mrs Brown has lost her handbag in Jubilee Park. Did anyone find a red leather bag with white spots today?'

'WAKKA WAK! No, I'm sorry,' said Mother Duck, who had her four tired ducklings under her wings. 'I didn't find a bag, but I did find this on the edge of the pond.' She pulled a pink plastic rattle from a pocket on her apron.

'Oh, we know who that rattle belongs to,' said Sulky the spider.

'Yes, we do,' whispered his sister Silky. 'It's that dear little baby with the red curly hair in the blue pram. He is a funny thing.'

'That's right,' said Brush Possum. 'His family had a picnic under our tree today.'

Then Sugar Possum said, 'His big sister had a fairy cake with pink icing and a glass of lemonade, and the baby ate a whole bowl of mashed apple.'

The four fat frogs agreed. They had seen the baby too. 'Yesterday he threw that same rattle into the water,' said the biggest frog.

'It fell right on my head,' said another. 'Erk! Look at the bump it gave me!'

But no-one had seen Mrs Brown's bag.

'Hurly-Burly,' exclaimed Pearlie. 'Babies are always losing things. We'll put the rattle in the Lost and Found box by the front gate and return it when we can.'

'Hmmm,' she thought to herself, 'these animals do see everything that happens in the park. They would make very good detectives.'

Pearlie asked everyone to get a good night's rest and all meet in the morning to have another look about.

That night, as she combed her long silver hair, Pearlie could not stop thinking about Mrs Brown.

'Oh dear, she will be worried,' thought Pearlie. 'I wonder what was in her bag? Probably her purse and her glasses. Perhaps she had to walk all the way home instead of catching the bus! Her poor, tired legs.'

Then Pearlie laid her head on her frilly blue pillow and tried to get some rest.

But what Pearlie did not know
was that the red spotty bag
was not lost. Those two bad
ratbags, Scrag and Mr Flea,
had taken Mrs Brown's
handbag and dragged it
through the park to their
hiding place underneath
a water tank.

CROWN PROPERTY

Scrag crawled inside the bag. 'Let's have a look what's in here,' he said. 'Hurrumph … there's nothing except this hankie. The purse must have fallen out!'

'Well, let's take the bag back then and get the reward,' squeaked Mr Flea.

'No, no, not yet!' growled Scrag. 'Can't you see? The longer we keep the bag the bigger the reward will be. We'll both be RICH!' Scrag laughed.

'Well, it's too dark to do anything now, I suppose,' said Mr Flea.

Scrag snarled at him, 'You can go and look for the purse first thing in the morning. Right now this lovely white hankie makes a very nice pillow.' He plonked his flea-bitten head on the handkerchief and Mr Flea joined him.

Soon both rats were fast asleep.

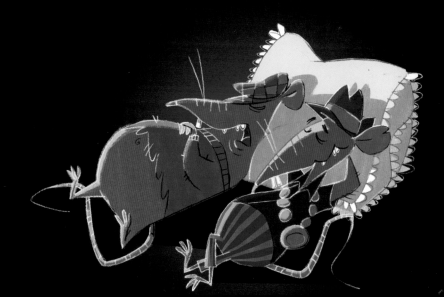

Next morning after breakfast all the animals gathered at the fountain ready to do their best to find Mrs Brown's bag.

There was a new sign on the lamppost:

Lost handbag

Red with white spots

Owner very upset

BIG reward

Ring Mrs Brown

0044 0044

'Reeds and ripples! This is just awful,' exclaimed Pearlie. 'Poor Mrs Brown. We must find that bag. I think that if we all work together we will have a better chance.'

'Today I want you all to look very hard for any clues,' she said. 'Mother Duck, you and your four babies waddle around the pond and see what you can find.

'Frogs, you have a look under the water.

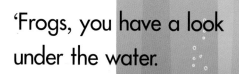

'Silky and Sulky, please use your eight eyes to see down in the long grass.

'And Brush and Sugar, your night eyes can search all the dark places. Let's meet back here this afternoon with anything we have seen.'

The animals were on the job immediately. They scattered in all directions.

Pearlie zoomed back to her shell and drew a large map of the park on the back of a paper bag.

While this was all happening, down under the water tank Scrag and Mr Flea were having another argument.

'I can't find the purse,' puffed Mr Flea, 'but I've just seen another sign. This time it says BIG reward. We should take the bag back now and get lots of money.'

'No, no, not yet!' Scrag shouted at him. 'If we keep it even longer, we will get lots MORE money. And then we will be VERY, VERY RICH!'

'Are you sure?' said Mr Flea as he scratched his head.

'YES,' cried Scrag. 'And by the way … would you like to chew on the bag for breakfast?'

'What does it taste like?' asked Mr Flea.

He took a big bite out of a handle.
'Delicious … BURP!'

And the two rotten rodents laughed loudly.

That afternoon Pearlie laid her map out on the grass. The animals all gathered around to tell Pearlie what they had seen.

The four fat frogs were very excited. 'Look at these, Pearlie,' the biggest frog said. 'A pair of eyeglasses with the letter "B" written on the side.'

'We found them in the mud. We think they're Mrs Brown's glasses,' said another frog.

Pearlie marked the spot where the glasses were found.

'We were looking in the long grass and we found a purse,' said Sulky. 'It was just there,' said Silky, pointing to the place on the map with her eight legs.

Pearlie flew to collect the purse. She knew it was Mrs Brown's because her library card was inside and so was a five-dollar note. Mrs Brown would be pleased to get her money back.

'We saw some tracks by the pond,' squawked Mother Duck. 'There were eight little footprints and it looked like they were dragging something between them.' Mother Duck showed Pearlie on the map where she saw the tracks.

playg

bench

mud

pond

hill

green house

Kiosk

long grass

water tank

Then it was the possums' turn to tell Pearlie what they had discovered. 'We heard some shouting from underneath the water tank,' said Sugar. 'And we saw Mr Flea running under there as fast as he could go,' said Brush.

Pearlie drew a big 'X' on the water tank. Now she knew exactly what had happened.

'Good work! Thank you, everyone,' said Pearlie.

'Someone *has* found Mrs Brown's bag and they will not give it back!'

'Oooh … errr,' everyone said. It was terrible to think such a thing could happen in Jubilee Park!

'Hurly-burly! Come on, everyone. Off we go,' Pearlie cried. She raced to the water tank with all the animals running behind.

When she got close Pearlie could hear voices. The two rats were fighting with each other again.

'I want the reward NOW,' yelled Mr Flea.

'I told you … just one more day and the reward will be even BIGGER,' cried Scrag.

Pearlie was very cross when she heard them. She rubbed her wings together and her green eyes flashed. She waved her magic wand. In the bright light she saw the two rats rolling around inside the bag.

'YOU BAD, BAD RATS!' shouted Pearlie. 'HAND OVER THAT BAG RIGHT NOW!'

'Oh, yes, yes, of course, Pearlie,' snivelled Mr Flea.

'We found it by the pond and we were just looking after it,' lied Scrag.

'I know what you were up to, you greedy villains!' cried Pearlie. 'You were keeping it for the reward. If you had given it back when you first found it you might have got a reward, but now you will get nothing!'

'I told him that,' said Mr Flea.

'It was just a mistake, Pearlie,' whimpered Scrag.

'For your punishment,' continued Pearlie, 'you will take everything in the Lost and Found box back to its owners. Start running, NOW!'

Scrag and Mr Flea tore off as fast as their skinny rat legs could take them.

Pearlie watched Scrag and Mr Flea pop a pink rattle back into the baby's blue pram. The baby's mother was most surprised to find it there.

They also returned a plastic cup to a family picnic set and a long-lost pen to a man's pocket without being seen at all.

Pearlie was very pleased. 'We all worked together to solve the crime,' she said. All the animals cheered, 'HOORAY!'

Pearlie flew with the bag back to her shell. She used her magic to clean off the mud and rat hair and to repair the chew marks. Soon the handbag looked as good as new.

Before long Pearlie saw Mrs Brown walking
slowly up the path, still searching high and
low for her bag.

Pearlie flew down to the pond and left it on a park bench where she would be sure to see it.

She hid and watched as Mrs Brown scooped up her precious bag. The dear old lady cried with happiness to find it safe and sound.

That night Pearlie hummed a lovely tune as she made herself a supper of fairy bread and daisy fizz. She didn't want money for her reward. She knew that the warm feeling she had inside was the best reward of all!